PSALM of a
Squealer's Brother

by Libya Freeman

Swan Publishing

ISBN: 978-1-936750-77-1

"The Lord is my shepherd; I shall not want...."

"I'm hungry!" cried Micah. The seven-year-old boy and his big brother, Jacob Thompson, surveyed the refrigerator. It was empty, as usual.

"Well," said Jacob, turning to face his sibling, "We'll just have to think."

"You think," Micah wisely replied, "I'll pray."

"Pray?" Jacob laughed. He was just about to mock the idea of praying on an empty stomach when he changed his mind. After all, he agreed, a little prayer wouldn't hurt.

Jacob sighed as his eyes scanned over their small, street-front home. It was as comfortable and orderly as he could make it, with its blue-painted kitchen seen straight through from the front door. The refrigerator was missing its handle. Only two of the four knobs remained on the stove top. The back door window hung a set of dingy, white curtains and a maple wood breakfast

1

table centered the room with three unmatched chairs. Jacob began touring the house. A short hallway led him into a bathroom draped with Christmas ornaments, though it was early Spring. His brother Derek's room held posters of favorite sports teams on every wall, while the night stand next to a headless board and bed held a silver-framed picture of their parents. Jacob moved to the second bedroom, belonging to Micah. It was also lacking. In a corner, there were few toys, a broken set of headphones and a race car bed that the youngster had nearly outgrown, but insisted on sleeping in every night. Jacob's and his brother's rooms were all neat and clean, but their living conditions were so below what he wanted for them, especially the neighborhood.

"I'll pray with you," voiced Jacob, returning to the front room and kneeling by the couch next to his brother now.

The child's prayer was a short one, which included the possibility of French fries, pizza, and cheeseburgers for dinner; while the elder silently prayed for food that would last them until his next pay check. Micah ended his prayer with a solemn "Amen." As the two stood, the kitchen door opened.

"Squirt, what are you doing on the floor?" The tone of the third voice entering jested. It was Derek, the middle brother.

Jacob walked toward the kitchen and probed the incoming athlete. "And where have you been?"

Derek laid his orange and black striped basketball on the table and answered, "Coach ended practice late."

"You don't have practice on Mondays," Jacob cross examined, as he removed the leather ball.

For a second, the scenario reminded Jacob of when his father was alive. Mr. Thompson had often corrected his oldest son for putting things on the table that didn't belong; the list of things included dirty laundry, sports gear, and video games.

"I wanted extra practice so I can get MVP," Derek explained. "I'm sorry, I didn't realize how late it was."

Jacob nodded his head. There was no reason to be upset, after all, the basketball captain was usually punctual. *It was just stress,* he resolved with a smile and shook off the bad feelings.

"So, what are we going to eat?" Derek inquired with a healthy appetitite.

"There isn't anything," informed Micah. "But it's okay," he added cheerily, "We prayed."

Derek smirked, but then after seeing his big brother's expression of encouragement, he nodded his head in unity. "Yep, prayer is good."

There was no food; that was that, Derek shrugged. Accepting the tough reality, yet persuaded to remain positive, the teenager suggested, "Let's watch TV. A friend let me borrow last Saturday's UFC match."

"I would ask which friend, but I don't think I want to know," It was hard for Jacob to resist being skeptical; yet, Derek ignored the remark.

The three brothers sat down and watched the fight. Halfway through the third round, a knock sounded. Jacob looked through the peep hole. It was Sister Moore, a church mother who dropped in occasionally to check on them. He opened the door narrowly and she stepped in, as usual.

"Hey Jacob, how are you doing, son? Are you still taking care of your brothers?"

"Uh, yes ma'am," Jacob answered carefully, as he followed her busy feet into the kitchen.

"The Lord just put ya'll on my heart. I thought you boys might be hungry, so I brought you some food."

"Food?" Micah asked excitedly, as Derek's eyes widened. The two smiled as they attentively watched the faithful member of their late grandmother's church.

"Yes, food. It's in my trunk." She handed Derek the keys to her car.

"Where is that mother of yours?" Sister Moore asked, as she poked around the house.

"Uh....She's around....But I haven't seen her lately," the guardian stuttered.

"I saw her...Three days ago." The short woman finally stood still. "I told that girl to come home," she added.

It was always interesting when people stuck their noses in places they didn't belong, thought Jacob, while he reflected upon his mother. His mother loved her children; but, after his father died four years ago, she mentally broke down. Leaving home for days at a time, she spent countless hours at the cemetery. It seemed to be her way of saying she had died too. Family and friends had convinced her to move in with her mother. The move helped and his mother improved for awhile. She started acting like a mom again; but, when their grandmother became ill and passed away shortly after, it appeared to be more than his mom could handle. She shriveled back into her shell and emotionally checked out of family life. Since that time, the children rarely saw their mother and her drifting visits left Micah bitterly weeping. So, Jacob took a job to care for his immediate family and now at twenty, he strove to keep them together.

"Well, here they are!" The short, stoutly woman spoke as the boys laid down the last over-loaded box of groceries on the kitchen floor.

"Sister Moore," Jacob muttered with his last ounce of dignity, "We can't accept all these boxes."

"Of course you can, you know my husband never had half a mind to run that store of his. Always over-ordering. Oh, there's one more thing in the car," she said, matter-of-factly.

"I'll get it!" Micah said, with no shame.

"It's in the front seat," Sister Moore spoke gloriously, "Sunday dinner!" Everybody who knew Sister Moore knew about her Sunday dinners. There was never any food left after she cooked. She was the best cook at their former church.

They glared at the steaming hot meal covered with aluminum foil .

"I have to go now," She said. "Brother Moore wants his dinner by the time he gets home from work."

The Thompson boys eyes followed Sister Moore as she drove away; then followed their noses toward their house, which now smelled like a bread factory.

Micah said a quick prayer of "Thank you's" and they ate the full course dinner of roast beef, mashed potatoes, green beans and yeast rolls, while they watched the rest of the fight. It was Monday, but Sunday's dinner never tasted so good.

"He makes me to lie down in green pastures; He leads me beside the still waters..."

T hings went well for the next few months. Jacob's supervisor had finally noticed his hard work and promoted him to Junior Manager. There is a limit to the positions available at fast food restaurants and the young man learned that none of them paid enough to support a family of three; but, Junior Manager was better than Janitor. Besides, the job had begun to get interesting. He was curious about one of the regular customers and wanted to know why it appeared that the mysterious man vanished from the counter whenever Jacob looked for him a second time. Recently, he had asked fellow workers about the stranger, but no one recalled. The man seemed so peculiar to Jacob and the escapade was starting to get creepy.

"I have a surprise," said Micah, running up to Jacob at the end of the first six weeks of school.

"What?" Asked Jacob, playing along with the guessing game.

"I have all 'A's' on my report card!"

"No, you don't," Jacob answered playfully. After reviewing the card, Jacob picked the wavy-haired boy up and spun him around. "Well, I'm happy someone is getting good grades." He put Micah down and glanced at his other brother.

The biggest problem Jacob had lately was Derek, who began to stay out late again. "Friends" was his excuse and the high school senior offered no specific names of his comrades. The school and the neighborhood were both reasons that "Friends" could mean trouble.

"How do you know I didn't get good grades?" Derek smirked as he laid his video game down.

"Well, go get your card," challenged Jacob.

Derek passed Jacob his grade card. Jacob observed it with surprise. The grades were all "A's," except for one "B" in Science. "I have to say, I'm shocked. I mean, this is definitely an improvement from last year."

Derek plopped back on the couch and continued to play.

"It's time for a celebration!" The perceptive brother declared. "Pizza and a movie."

"I'll get my shoes," Micah exclaimed, running to his room before Jacob could change his mind.

"Now?" Frowned Derek, unexcited.

"You can save the game," Jacob replied.

"Whatever!" Derek mumbled under his breath and rose from the couch.

Yes, thought Jacob, *Everything is going to be fine, when his brother fixed his rotten attitude.*

During dinner, Derek talked about basketball and how everyone on the team was competing over the award of the year. They all wanted it-especially Trey. All of the guys on Derek's team sounded like thugs, as Jacob listened; particularly the kid named Trey. But Derek didn't notice Jacob's concern, he just continued on about the award.

The elder brother remembered the annual award. He had wanted it himself when he was on the varsity team. It was a special award for the community kids, because, whoever received it was also given an opportunity to be recognized by basketball scouts. If a scout saw professional potential in an MVP, then that could mean more money and a ticket out of their poor neighborhood. Coach David had connections with the big leagues and utilized his associations for the betterment of his teamsters. The coach desired to see the children in the community do better for themselves by becoming more cultured and well rounded. Jacob's father and Coach David had been friends for a long time.

His father was all Jacob had needed to keep him grounded.

Later, as he stared into the bathroom mirror, Jacob realized he was turning into his father. Tall with curly, trimmed hair, the lean young man of dark-chocolate skin and athletic build invited many compliments from females. Even his voice sounded like his father's. These were some of the contributing factors that kept his mom away, Jacob was sure. He remembered her crying one night after she returned. "I just loved him too much," she said, as he held her. He walked to the bedroom wishing she was there loving them now.

"He restores my soul; He leads me in the paths of righteousness for His name's sake..."

"Amen!" Shouted Jacob. He was at a church service. It wasn't the church he had grown up in with his parents and grandmother. No, this was a new church, a church for him. After his grandmother passed, he realized it was time to move on. He found a place that he and his brothers loved. Not only was Jacob enjoying coming to church, but he understood more what was being said.

After a couple more "Amens" from the congregation, the pastor dismissed them to greetings. The Thompson boys were interrupted by a voice from behind, "Jacob!"

They all turned to watch Pastor Dan walk toward Jacob. "Yes sir?" The young man responded.

I noticed you in the congregation. You and your brothers here seem to be the only young ones listening."

"It was a great sermon. I'm sure everyone enjoyed it."

"I would like to talk to you later. I am looking for someone to help our youth. They seem so bored and uninterested," said Pastor Dan, concerned. "Maybe we can meet sometime and talk."

"Sure, that would be fine."

"Thank you, son," replied the pastor, just before being swept away by a crowd of members discussing his sermon.

As Jacob drove home, he wondered. How did the pastor know his name? What did the pastor want him to do about the disinterest? What could he do, seeing he was just as disinterested as this group was not so long ago?

When he pulled to the front of his house, there were boys hanging around the porch. They were all about Derek's age and were dressed in one color; signifying one thing in the neighborhood, gang.

"Who are they?" Micah questioned.

"Uh…Those are just my friends," answered Derek nervously.

"*Those* are the friends you've been hanging out with?" Inquired Jacob, displeased.

"Well, yeah. They're my friends; we're going to play some ball."

"Try again," corrected Jacob, crawling out of the car.

Micah got out on Jacob's side and stood next to him.

"Will you cut it out?" Derek sharply whispered, attempting to quieten his brother.

Jacob walked with Micah toward the house while Derek stopped to talk with his friends.

"What's up, fellas; how are you doing?" Greeted Jacob, stepping onto the porch.

"Aw, we're fine," said one of the guys, slowly. He had an attitude that would only belong to the leader.

"Hey, what's that behind you?" The visitor jokingly referred to Micah, who was hiding behind his oldest brother.

"He's my brother," said Derek, looking to be in some kind of stage between nervousness and panic.

"Why is he standing behind him?" He teased. "My name is Trey, little man, what's yours?"

Micah didn't respond. He just stood closer to Jacob.

Jacob gave Derek a look that meant "You'd better be home by curfew," at which Derek nodded.

As Jacob tucked Micah in that night, he realized why that group bothered him. It was their leader Trey. He remembered Trey was a cousin of Jacob's former best friend, Andrew.

Jacob and Andrew had been as close as brothers. Mr. Thompson was like a father to the boy who lived a few blocks away. Jacob had met Andrew at his grandmother's church. The two played in the community together, mowed lawns as partners and were on the same basketball team. During work or play, they were together; until Jacob's father passed. Then, Andrew took a wrong turn back down the road of drugs and quick money. Jacob followed, believing that a career in fast food wasn't going to suffice a family of fast growing, hungry boys. So, he involved himself in a few drug deals. But Jacob soon grew to understand that his responsibility to his brothers was greater than he realized; he was exposing his brothers to the streets. Andrew parted furiously at the decision and there had been no more communication between the two.

But, it was too late. Derek had already caught the back end of the friendship and began to hang out with Andrew's younger cousin, Devin. Now, Derek and Devin were inseparable.

Jacob had agreed to let the two younger boys hang out together. As long as they were there at the Thompson house where he could keep his eye on them, he hoped it would be harmless. But, now it was clear to Jacob, after seeing Devin and Trey with the other members of the gang, that the two boys related to Andrew were up to no good.

Jacob met with Pastor Dan. The pastor quickly put him to work and set up a youth devotion. The teens could talk truthfully about their thoughts and lives; nothing was forbidden. The group suddenly exploded with activity and increased with young people from the community. Pastor Dan saw the change and was thrilled. The Thompson boys learned more about the pastor and his wife and grew closer to their church leaders. The pastors learned about the boys' situation and often reminded them that his door was always open.

As the brothers left Pastor Dan's house one evening, Micah asked Derek if their church shepherd was what having a father was like, because it had seemed so long ago since the little boy remembered his dad.

"Yep," Derek replied. "That's just what a father is like."

*"Yea, though I walk through
the valley of the shadow
of death, I will fear no evil;
for You are with me; Your rod
and staff, they comfort me..."*

J acob opened his front door and was welcomed
by three of his brother's friends. "Where's
Micah?" He questioned, suddenly feeling much
older as he walked into the kitchen. At the sound
of giggles from a back room, Jacob smiled.
Micah's laughter made his heart glad. He walked
to Micah's room and stood in the doorway. A
young man whose back was turned was tickling
his brother. Jacob observed that the familiar body
was larger than most of Derek's friends. Micah
and the tickler turned to face Jacob.

"Hey, big bro." Andrew said, now standing.
"How've you been? I haven't seen you in a year
or two."

Jacob nodded his head tensely. "I've been
well."

"Still struggling, I see." Sighed Andrew, smartly. "I wish you would've just taken my help and weren't so stubborn."

Jacob motioned for Micah to come to him while Andrew continued talking.

There was a long silence and Micah found his way out of the room.

"Always so nice, Jake... I just came to see if the Thompson brothers had changed. You know, Micah still remembers me a little. He had no problem letting me in the front door."

"Yeah, well that's because I haven't told them what you started doing."

"You mean what I always did? The way I made money suddenly became a problem for you."

Jacob was silent.

"It's okay, I won't hold it against you."

Jacob didn't like the way things were turning out.

"I'd like you to leave."

"No can do," smirked Andrew. "I'm watching my cuz. I think he's starting to take after me."

Jacob couldn't believe his day. He tried his best not to aggravate Andrew and his family, but he knew they were trouble, more trouble than Derek could understand. After dinner, Jacob tried to explain to Derek without too much detail why the neighborhood boys were no longer welcome in their home, but his brother didn't agree.

Micah also held firm, innocently. "But Andrew is still our friend. He isn't bad."

"I'm just saying, watch out for them and do not let them back in this house."

"Or what?" asked Derek. "Since when do you tell us who we can hang out with? You are not our dad!"

Jacob icily stared at his brother. "I don't care, I've always taken care of you and since when did you stop listening to good advice? Could it be since Devin has been talking to you…Telling you what you don't have? How much farther along you could be if you do what his cousins do? That stuff will get you arrested or killed. I don't want to see you hanging out with them again." Jacob stormed into his room and slammed the door. He was too young to deal with this, he thought, as he tiredly dropped onto his bed.

Later that night, Jacob awoke and told his brothers the whole story about he and Andrew. He realized it was the only way to make them understand.

After prayer and time, Derek finally saw the light and obeyed Jacob. He worked hard in school and basketball practice. He avoided Devin and and his group when he could, but it was causing a split between him and the team mates who sided with Trey. Nobody did anything that would alert the coach, but Coach David noticed anyway. He eventually called Derek and Devin into his office after practice.

"I sense tension," he eyed Derek. "I know what extracurricular activities go on in this neighborhood," continued the slightly bald man, "but I also remember young Jake Thompson. You'd be wise to follow in his footsteps."

Devin laughed a little as they walked outside. "He needs to stay out of my business."

"Maybe you and your cousins shouldn't run your business across the street from the school."

"Man, I thought you were cooler than your punk brother."

Derek stopped walking and waited for Devin to face him. "Don't you want more than this, man?"

"Living the streets, ruling the streets, that's what I'm living for," Devin answered, proudly.

Derek shook his head, "I see the way you all look at me and I hear what you say. Just because I refuse to be like you, dress like you or talk like you; you call me a 'white boy.' I don't care, I'm going somewhere."

Devin nodded his head, his face looked sad for a moment. He turned and walked away raising his finger derogatively. It was a sign that they were over as friends.

Micah tossed and turned. He dreamed his mom had come home, only to leave again. Later, he had a rough day at school. He saw Andrew giving things to kids on the school grounds. He knew what the small packages were, but he didn't say anything. Andrew scared him. When the young man had asked to come inside their house, he had told the child that he was his brother's close friend. He lied. Micah didn't want to see him again. He didn't like people getting him into trouble. The next morning at school, Micah told the principle what he had seen. The principle alerted the authorities and Micah watched as they talked amidst themselves. Micah began to feel afraid. He didn't know why so many officials were stirring about after what he'd said.

When Jacob came to the school, he was upset. Micah weakly smiled at him in the principal's office and hoped that he wasn't in trouble. Jacob passed him and went into the office to talk with the principal. When he came out, he gave Micah a huge hug and kiss and told him he acted very courageously.

When the two brothers arrived home from school, Andrew, Trey, and several other boys were lounging around the Thompson's front porch again. Jacob attempted to walk directly into his house, but as he turned the door knob, Trey grabbed his arm. Micah shrunk behind his two bigger brothers.

"Hey, what's wrong, Micah? Suddenly, you don't talk."

"He talks," defended Jacob calmly. "Now, I suggest you let go of my arm."

Trey laughed.

"Uh…May I get into my house?" Jacob continued, wanting to leave before things became more heated.

"You go in your house," said Andrew.

As soon as the door opened, Micah ran inside.

Andrew took a deep breath. "Bro, we need to talk about Micah. It seems he likes to talk at all the wrong times."

Jacob frowned and motioned his other brother to go inside.

"Hey Derek, don't go anywhere, I want to talk to you," ordered Trey.

Get off my property," demanded Jacob, angrily.

"I thought we were all friends," mocked Andrew.

"No," replied Jacob. "You all are Juvenile Court's friends."

"Listen, my advice to you is to keep your brother's mouth shut so we won't have any problems. We go way back; we shouldn't have to be dealin' with this."

"My advice to you is stay away from my brothers." Jacob shot back, then walked into the house and locked the door.

They had attempted to put Andrew away before. There were so many drug charges and so few witnesses. When people realized a seven-year-old boy had this much courage, others decided to do the same. Andrew was the center of a drug chain and there were a lot worse people who he was connected to in the neighborhood; but, people grew tired of being afraid. They stood up and Andrew was justly prosecuted.

Jacob rolled over and pounded his clock. It was five A.M. and although his body was used to waking up, he was dog tired. Micah had woken up twice through the night with nightmares; this time in fear of Andrew. He had finally fallen asleep in Jacob's bed. Jacob rose out of the bed as quietly as he could. The last thing he wanted was for Micah to wake up. As he walked to the bathroom, he heard a whistle outside. He walked over to the slightly opened window. Suddenly, he saw one of the thugs he had seen around the neighborhood whose name was Mike. At that moment, Mike lit a match. Jacob didn't wait to see what Mike was going to do with the match; he knew gasoline when he smelled it. He ran to the bed and picked up Micah.

"Derek!" Jacob yelled at his other brother who was normally hard to awaken. He pushed open Derek's door with his foot while still balancing Micah in his arms.

"Wake-" Jacob looked at Derek and his bed. Derek was already awake and stuffing things into two backpacks. Jacob signaled him with his head to get up. They exited Derek's room and were headed toward the kitchen door when they heard the window glass break in Jacob's room. It only took a second for the sound of flames to follow. They rushed out of the back door as more glass shattered. They raced around the front of the house. There was no sound to be heard in the neighborhood and no one was around anywhere.

"The keys!" moaned Jacob. "I forgot the car keys!"

Derek pulled the set of keys out of his pants pocket. They jumped in the car and Jacob quickly sat Micah in the back seat.

"Where are we going?" Asked Micah sleepily.

"We are going to Pastor's house," answered Jacob as he backed out of the driveway onto the road and sped off. Jacob instructed Micah to dial 911 on his cell phone.

As he drove, the elder brother wondered how in the world his life had gotten this messy. At first, his family was on its way out of the bad neighborhood and things were finally getting better. He had graduated second in his class and was going to college with a full academic scholarship; but, suddenly his father died, his mother's troubles started and then his grandmother died. Now, he was working overtime in a fast food restaurant to support his family and they were living in his grandmother's house. His life had made a U-turn.

As he pulled into Pastor Dan's driveway, the sky had just begun to lighten. He noticed a car in the driveway that belonged to Mrs. Murray, the church secretary. He wondered why she was at his house this early. Jacob got out of the car and shut the door quietly because Micah and Derek were both asleep now. He shook his head. Derek had a lot of nerve going to sleep when his "friends" were the ones causing this mess. He rang the doorbell and Mrs. Murray answered. "Jacob, what are you doing here?

"Some of Derek's buddies are burning down our house," he answered hastily.

"What?" She froze in shock.

"Is pastor home?" Jacob asked.

"No honey, his wife is though," Mrs. Murray answered and called for the pastor's wife.

"What are you going to do?" Inquired Mrs. Murray?

"I don't know. I can't let Derek or Micah go to school."

"I can take care of them," the secretary said to the boys and pastor's wife.

"No, I can't ask you to do that, Sister Murray."

"You have a job to go to, don't you?" She asked.

The young man nodded.

"Well, I'll take them. Micah can help me with church filing and Derek can clean up; Lord knows I need the help."

Jacob thought about it. If he didn't work, they didn't eat. He couldn't afford to take a day off and there were Derek's friends.

"I will take you up on that offer, but I don't know what those punks are going to do next; they're dangerous."

"I'm taking them," Mrs. Murray boldly insisted. "You go on to work."

He hesitated, but she reassured him. "Honey, don't worry. I'm not saved to the bone yet; so, The Bible isn't the only thing I'm packing."

The thought of Sister Murray with a weapon was scary to Jacob. He hoped for their sakes the thugs would stay away. Jacob loaded Micah into Mrs. Murray's car, told him to be good, and gave him a kiss. He pulled Derek out. "Now, you listen to her and do not do anything foolish."

Jacob watched Derek slowly get into Mrs. Murray's car as he drove away.

"You prepare a table before me in the presence of my enemies; You anoint my head with oil; my cup runs over..."

J acob started his car; but, instead of it cranking he heard a terrible "clank." He had just gotten off work and phoned Mrs. Murray to let her know he was on his way to pick up his brothers. She had asked him how he was and he said fine. It wasn't exactly the truth. The police had been by to talk to him. He told them his story. They nodded their heads and listened; but, Jacob could tell they were skeptical. He had hopped into his car and left the scene, instead of waiting for the fire department to arrive. He wasn't about to stick around and had told them so.

The house was badly burned...Jacob's room was completely gone...Micah's and Derek's room were slightly damaged; but, some of the furniture in the house had been saved...The house was covered by insurance...A fire-proof safe was found in the attic. The police officer was reciting the facts of the incident to Jacob, but he was oblivious by the distraction of the mysterious customer. The man was outside, this time peering through the window. As Jacob sat in his manager's office and talked with the police, he could see the customer watching him through the black tint. A few minutes later, he saw a double silhouette of the man on the wall.

"Mr. Thompson?" The police officer interrupted.

I am becoming way too paranoid. Jacob blinked to recover his focus.

"Well, I think that is all for now. We'll contact you if we get more information and call us if you need us." The policeman departed and Jacob's manager stepped inside.

"Why didn't you say anything?"

"Come on," said his boss. "I would have given you the day off: I would have given you the month off."

Jacob sat quietly.

"Well, if you're not going to say anything, you can get back to work."

Jacob slowly rose from his chair. He did the rest of his work as if he were sleep-walking. It was all like a nightmare. As he worked, the thugs entered the restaurant and took a seat in the back. They did not order any food; they just stared at Jacob, attempting to intimidate him. Meanwhile, the mysterious man visited Jacob as he sat down during his lunch break. The customer stood in front of him, then sat. "How are you, young man?"

"Good," answered Jacob as he bit into his sandwich.

"How are you feeling? I know it's been a long day."

"How would you know?" Asked Jacob, tensely. "Are you spying on me?"

"Jacob, you should calm yourself," said the man. "Let's start over, my name is Grey."

"Well, Grey, since you probably already know my name, it only leaves one question; what do you want?"

Grey was silent and almost seemed to disappear.

"Listen," said Jacob, "I'm sorry, but I don't know you and I don't know what you know about me." He couldn't be too careful these days with all that was happening to him. Jacob looked closely into Grey's face which hid beneath a gray cap with a faded white emblem. Grey's cloudy, gray eyes suddenly transformed into piercing blue.

The man smiled, "I've come to give you a word of encouragement. It looks like you really need one."

Jacob marveled and felt the urge to listen intently, despite his tiredness.

"Faith."

Jacob waited for more. After a few seconds, he frowned. "That's it?"

" I did say a *word* of encouragement."

"So...Could you elaborate a little?" He observed the strange man's warm smile.

"What am I supposed to have faith in?"

"God," answered Grey.

"Ok..." This conversation was seemingly pointless and Jacob began to think Grey was a nutcase. "I have faith in God," he continued.

"Fine." Grey rose from his seat.

"Well, this is something."

"Jacob Thompson isn't thinking with faith," Grey added.

"No, I don't feel like thinking at all. Today has been hard and I don't know what's next." Jacob looked at his food; he wasn't really hungry anymore.

"Faith. Faith in what you know can happen. You say you trust Him to protect you and your brothers, but you don't. It is just something to say to comfort yourself while carrying the world on your shoulders. You have to have faith that things will turn out like you have asked. Let your worries go. You can't fix your problems so why do you worry? He can fix them, if you let him."

Jacob sighed. The message wasn't exactly joyful, but he knew Grey was right.

"Thank you," said Jacob, now standing. "I… needed that."

"No problem," said Grey smiling. "I actually have to go now," said Grey, checking his watch.

"Thanks again," Jacob repeated.

Grey smiled again and walked away. Jacob went back to work then watched Grey approach the boys in the back of the room and talk to them. A few minutes later they left.

"Surely goodness and mercy shall follow me all the days of my life;"

The ride Jacob took to the church seemed longer than usual. There was a lot of traffic, but he didn't mind. When he arrived at the church, Derek was cleaning the floors. Jacob watched a moment. "Hey bro," said Jacob, laughing. "Are you having fun?"

"Tons," replied Derek, grinning.

"Where's Mrs. Murray?

"She's in the pastor's office."

"Where's Micah?"

"He's in there too."

Jacob walked into his pastor's office. Mrs. Murray and the pastor were huddled around the young techni-brain.

"I wondered what that icon was for," said Sister Murray, smiling.

"Hey Micah, what's up, bud?" Jacob spoke.

Micah ran to Jacob.

"Your brother is just showing us how to use the computer," said Mrs. Murray, impressed.

"Jacob, your brother is brilliant," agreed Pastor Dan, rising from his chair.

"Thank you." Jacob was glad that at least Micah was worry free.

"Jacob, do you want to talk?" Asked Pastor Dan.

Mrs. Murray excused herself and Micah from the room as Jacob began to tell the Pastor what happened. Pastor Dan insisted Jacob and his brothers stay with him, but Jacob refused. He knew Micah and Derek could be pretty carefree in other people's houses. After a prayer and a note of caution, The church leader released the family from his office.

As they rode in the car, Jacob noticed how quiet Derek was. He guessed it was because his teenage brother was trying to come up with a story to explain how he knew about the fire. Derek had packed some of their most treasured keepsakes in his bags that morning. Jacob assumed that someone in the group must have let Derek know ahead of time.

"I don't want to know why you knew. But I'm thankful." Jacob broke the silence. "You're okay, little brother. I know you'll turn into a good man just like dad."

Jacob hoped that he could comfort his brother, but instead, Derek continued his silence.

"What's wrong?" Asked Jacob, concerned.

"He wants to play in the game tonight," Micah answered for his brother.

"What game?"

"The championship game is tonight," he continued in his brother's interest.

"Shut up!" Interrupted Derek. He knew how stupid it would be to go when they could be in danger.

Andrew had made his position clear by terrorizing them, "Keep silent." Micah and his brothers had not followed the normal rule of conduct for the 'hood.'

The rest of the trip to the hotel was silent. They checked in and as soon as they saw the two beds, the boys dived in. Both his brothers began to laugh and play, but Jacob didn't hear them. As soon as he hit the full-sized mattress, he was out like a lamp. An hour later, Jacob woke up with a lot on his mind. He had tried hard to do things by himself. What was he thinking raising two boys at his age? He had refused the help of many family members to intervene. He had promised his father that he would be strong and tried to keep his word. He glanced at Micah watching TV and Derek sitting on the end of the other bed silently.

He decided what would be best for their future. "Alright," now he spoke concerning their present circumstances, "Get your shoes on; we're going to the game." After all, it was Derek's last game of the season.

Jacob sat at the game with Micah on his right side. All the thugs in Trey's crew were at the game. Jacob had forgotten that they were players; *I knew this was a dumb idea.*

Derek and his team won the game. Seventy-six to seventy-two, with Derek and Devin taking the glory for the final play. At the end of the game, Jacob was ready to go and was taking all precautions.

Immediately, everything in the gym turned dark. Spotlights whirled around and finally stopped at Derek's coach. Jacob, smiled, remembering this routine was normal for the last game of the season.

"Everyone knows we give out awards at this time. I've got some great boys on my team," spoke the coach as he began to hand out awards to several players. Then, Coach David announced that he was giving his favorite award, the Most Valuable Player. The person who won this award was credited for his athletic ability throughout the season, as well as his academic achievements. He had developed a good attitude and was an inspiration to all the team. This person was considered to be an all-around good athlete. The coach paused a second for a dramatic effect, then called Derek's name. Everyone cheered and Jacob was happy his brother won; but, when he watched Andrew angrily rise from the bench and exit the gym, his stomach tensed in dread. Jacob sought to get Derek safely home as soon as possible. He looked to his side for his little brother. Micah had run to Derek amid the excited crowd. Jacob could only think about the gang. He pushed his way through the mass of people, looking right and left; up and down into the bleachers. Micah wasn't very tall, so he could easily be overlooked. Jacob reached Derek, then felt a tap on his shoulder. He turned to see Grey, who had led Micah by the hand. Jacob pulled Micah to him. "Thank God!"

He didn't know why Grey was here, but he was extremely glad. When Jacob looked up to thank Grey, the old man was gone.

"And I will dwell in the house of the Lord forever."
Psalm 23

"Let's go!" Jacob yelled, while he loaded their last packed bags. The house was cleared of everything they wanted. Jacob closed the back lid of their new truck and walked to the front door.

As Micah walked out, he whined, "I don't want to move."

"You'll like it in Oklahoma," replied Jacob. "There's a lot of land."

"So? "What do I care about land?" He insisted.

"Because it's a lot of space for you to run around; plus, we'll be living with family.

"Dad's family," added Derek, whose position was neutral. As long as there was a basketball and goal around, he knew he would enjoy the place.

"I don't know them," frowned Micah.

"Well, we know them and they're nice, so come on," settled Jacob.

They reached the truck and climbed in. Without looking back, Jacob pulled off.

Jacob had seen his mom before they left and told her where she could visit them. As he drove down the street, he passed a group of thugs watching him. He was leaving, he thought. He didn't care if they were watching. At the speed he was going, it only took him ten minutes to get onto the interstate.

Storms were clearing for The Thompson Family. Jacob marveled as they destined out of state. If there had not been chaos, he would not be driven to move, nor would he had known of the money stashed in his grandmother's attic. Now, they were set on the road to a new beginning. The day after Derek's graduation he told his brothers about the move. There was family in Oklahoma; there was safety. He apologized to them for being foolish. They would have done better by moving sooner. A job was waiting. Their family owned a chain of successful restaurants and he accepted a position with prospects of finishing school and part ownership. He had prayed hard and hoped everything worked out. Just thinking about it again made Jacob start to pray.

"All the stations in Oklahoma are Cowboys, aren't they?" Micah asked, while listenening to his new radio with matching green headphones.

"Huh?" Jacob's thoughts were interrupted.

"All the radio stations," repeated Micah, "They're all Cowboy, aren't they?"

Jacob laughed. "No, the radio stations are all different just like in Memphis."

Micah seemed a little comforted about that and sat quietly.

"We have a lot of cousins your age. They're all very nice and won't tease you. Uncle Billy and Aunt Jackie have horses." said Derek. Anything problematic in their lives had little to no effect on Derek.

The concerns Micah expressed about their new destination were slowly disappearing. Jacob was relieved as they arrived on the other side of the bridge. He filled up the gas tank and as he got back in the vehicle, his pocket vibrated. It was a text message on his cell phone from Pastor Dan. He leaned back and read it.

"I hope you're driving the speed limit. Remember your Angels, Goodness and Mercy are following you. Be safe. You're in my prayers. Also, I have a friend in Oklahoma; a young pastor who needs help with his youth. Think and pray about it. Dan."

"That was a long text," said Derek, reading over Jacob's shoulder. "He couldn't have just called?"

Jacob started the engine and began to drive.

The sign read "Ten miles to Oklahoma." Jacob hoped this was a right move. Pastor Dan's text was nice. He had prayed for protection, but felt he needed a sign; to know they were safe and being guided.

As he tried to change over to the next lane, he noticed a gray car to the right of him with a white emblem on its license plate which was a halo. As Jacob slowed down, the car sped up to allow its tail end to be seen. The license plate read, "Goodness."

He looked to the left and saw another gray car of the same model and emblem. He didn't have to look at the license plate to know that it read, "Mercy."

Selah

"Thank You for Reading This Book.
We Hope You Enjoyed the Content of Its Pages.
Swan Publishing

CPSIA information can be obtained at www.ICGtesting.com
Printed in the USA
LVOW071706130712

289966LV00001B/24/P